321370

William's Dragons

by
Alan Baker

D1355040

FALKIRK COUNCIL
LIBRARY SUPPORT
FOR SCHOOLS

meadowside
CHILDREN'S BOOKS

The last thing...

...that William expected,

as he walked beyond
the garden,
and into
the woods…

…was to find a
tiny lizard…

…lazing in the sun
by a pond.

But then the lizard
changed into a
beautiful dragon.

William climbed onto its back
and they flew
up…

…and up…

…and up…

...high above the clouds
towards the mountains.

They found themselves at the
mouth of a cave.

Inside were creatures of
all shapes and sizes…

…and there was the Glump.

William found

some steps...

...and slowly climbed...

...up the steps that curled around the mountain.

At the top he made a
flag out of his scarf…

…but the snow began to
crumble and he slipped…

…tumbling down…

…and down…

…until he landed in the pond
at the bottom of
the garden…

...where he found a
lizard, lazing in the sun.

"I wonder where my scarf is?"
thought William.

FALKIRK COUNCIL
LIBRARY SUPPORT
FOR SCHOOLS

To my Mum with love
A.B.

Meadowside Children's Books
185 Fleet Street
London
EC4A 2HS

This edition first published 2006
Text and illustrations © Alan Baker 2006
The right of Alan Baker to be identified as the author
and illustrator has been asserted by him in accordance
with the Copyright, Designs and Patents Act, 1988

A CIP catalogue record for this book is available
from the British Library
10 9 8 7 6 5 4 3 2 1
Printed in China